P9-APU-117

Enid Blyton's

Christmas in the Toyshop

A Templar Book

Produced by The Templar Company plc
Pippbrook Mill, London Road, Dorking, Surrey RH4 1JE, Great Britain

First published as *Oh! What a Lovely Time* by
The Brockhampton Press Ltd in 1949

This edition published 1990 by Gallery Books,
an imprint of W.H. Smith Publishers, Inc.,
112 Madison Avenue, New York, New York 10016.
Gallery Books are available for bulk purchase for sales
promotions and premium use.
For details write or telephone the Manager of Special Sales,
W.H. Smith Publishers, Inc., 112 Madison Avenue,
New York, New York 10016. (212) 532-6600
First published in Canada 1990 by
W.H. Smith Ltd, 113 Merton Street, Toronto,
Canada M45 1A8

ISBN 0-8317-1291-0

Color separations by Positive Colour Ltd, Maldon, Essex, Great Britain
Printed and bound by L.E.G.O., Vicenza, Italy

Enid Blyton's

Christmas in the Toyshop

Illustrated by Sue Pearson

GALLERY BOOKS
An Imprint of W. H. Smith Publishers Inc.
112 Madison Avenue
New York City 10016

Once upon a time there was a toy shop. It sold candy as well as toys, so it was a very nice shop indeed.

All the children loved it. They used to come each day and press their noses against the window, and look in to see what toys there were.

"Oh look at that beautiful doll!" they would say. "Oh, do you see that train with its three cars – and it's got tracks to run on too."

"Look at the rocking-horse. I do love his friendly face!"

"Oh, what a lovely shop this is! When we grow up let's have a shop *just* like this one!"

Miss Roundy, the shopkeeper, liked having a toy shop. She liked seeing the children and showing them all her toys, and she nearly always gave them an extra candy or two in their bags when they came to spend their pocket money. So, of course, the children all loved her.

The toys loved her, too.

"Look – she found me a new key when mine dropped behind the shelf and couldn't be found," said the wind-up train.

"And she put a spot of red paint on my coat where some got rubbed off," said one of the toy soldiers. "She's very, very kind."

The toys liked living in Miss Roundy's shop until they were bought by the children. It was fun to sit on the shelves and the counter and watch the boys and girls come in and hear them talk. And it was very exciting when one of them was bought and taken proudly away by a child.

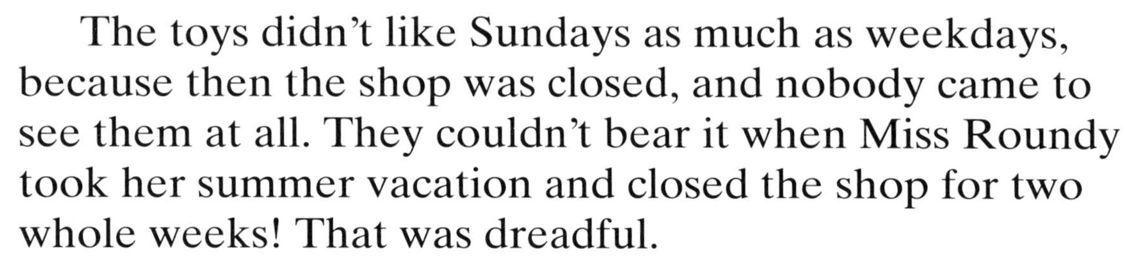

The toys didn't like Sundays as much as weekdays, because then the shop was closed, and nobody came to see them at all. They couldn't bear it when Miss Roundy took her summer vacation and closed the shop for two whole weeks! That was dreadful.

"It's so *dull*," complained the biggest teddy bear, and he pressed his middle to make himself growl mournfully. "There's no one to see and nothing to do. Miss Roundy even pulls down the window shade so that we can't see the children looking in at us."

And then Christmas time came, and the toys had a shock. Miss Roundy was going to close the shop for four whole days and go away to stay with her aunt. Oh dear!

"Four days of dullness and quietness and darkness," said the rocking horse, gloomily. "Nothing to do. No one to come and buy us, or see how nice we are. Four whole days!"

A black monkey with a red ribbon around his neck

spoke in a high, chattering voice.

"Can't we have a Christmas party for ourselves?"

"It's an idea," said the rocking horse, smiling. "Let's all think about it until Christmas comes – then we'll have a GRAND time in here by ourselves!"

The day came when Miss Roundy was going to close the shop. She pulled down the big window shade. Then she turned to the watching toys.

"I'm going now, toys," she said. "I won't see you again for four whole days. Be good. Merry Christmas to you – and try and have a good time yourselves. Do what you like – *I* won't mind! Merry Christmas!"

She went out of the shop and locked the door. The toys heard her foot-steps going down the street.

"Merry Christmas, Miss Roundy!" said everyone, softly. "You're nice!"

And now they were all alone for four days. *What* were they going to do?

The toys did what they always did as soon as the shop was closed for the night. They got up and stretched themselves, because they got stiff with sitting so long on the shelves and counter.

"That's better," said the rag doll, shaking out her legs one after the other to loosen them.

The pink cat rolled over and over. "Ah – that was good," she said, standing up again. "I love a roll."

The little wind-up train whistled loudly and the toy soldiers climbed out of their boxes and began marching back and forth.

"Nice to stretch our legs a little," they said, and then they scattered because the roly-poly man came rolling along, not looking where he was going, as usual.

"Look out," cried the captain of the soldiers, "you'll bump into the doll house! There he goes, rolling here and there – what a way to get around!"

"Listen, everyone!" called the rocking horse. "Let's talk about Christmas."

"When is it?" asked the big teddy bear.

"The day after tomorrow," said the rocking horse. "I think if we're going to have a good Christmas ourselves, we ought to make our plans now and get everything going, so that we're ready by Christmas Day."

"Oh yes!" cried everyone, and they all gathered around the rocking horse. What a crowd there was. All the little doll house dolls, and the other bigger dolls, the skittles, the wind-up train with its cars, and another wooden train, and the roly-poly man, and … well, I couldn't possibly tell you all of them, but you know what toys there are in a toy shop, don't you?

"Sit down," said the rocking horse. And everyone sat, except, of course, the things that could only stand, like the trains and the motor cars and the balls.

"We want a party," said the rocking horse. "That means we must have things to eat. We can take as much of the candy as we like, to make into cakes and things – Miss Roundy said we could help ourselves."

"We can make the food," said the doll house dolls.

"We'll help," said the skittles, excitedly.

"We can cook on that nice toy stove over there," said the twin dolls. One of the twins was a boy doll and the other was a girl doll, and they were exactly alike.

"The pink cat and the black monkey can arrange the circus," said the rocking horse. "They'll have lots of fun working together on that."

"I'll do the Christmas tree," said the wind-up sailor. "We'll have presents for everyone under it! We'll play games afterwards, too."

"What a pity Santa Claus doesn't know about us!" said the roly-poly man. "It would be so nice if he came to the party."

"I don't suppose he'll be able to come," said the black monkey. "He's much too busy at Christmas time. Don't roll against me like that, roly-poly man. You'll knock me over."

The roly-poly man rolled away and bumped into a row of soldiers. They went down on the floor at once. As they got up and brushed themselves off, they shouted angrily at the roly-poly man.

"Let's not quarrel," said the rocking horse. "People should never quarrel at Christmas time. It's a time to make one another happy and glad. Now – to your work, everyone – and we'll see what a wonderful Christmas Day we will have!"

The dolls and the skittles went to work at once. The doll with golden hair and the twin dolls took charge of

the cooking. They got the little toy stove going, and there was soon a *most* delicious smell in the toy shop – the cakes were baking!

There were chocolate cakes and fudge cakes and peppermints. There were little jellies made of the jelly candy Miss Roundy sold. There was a very big iced cake with tiny candles on it that the rag doll had found in a box.

The baking and cooking went on all day long. The twin dolls had to scold the roly-poly man many times because he kept rolling against the golden-haired doll just as she was taking the cakes out of the oven.

Still, as you can see, there was plenty of everything.

"What a feast we are going to have!" said the rag doll, greedily. "Ooooh – fudge cakes – I'll have six of those, please, on Christmas Day!"

The wind-up sailor did the Christmas tree. He was very, very clever. He climbed right up to the highest shelf, which Miss Roundy had decorated with evergreens, and he chose a very nice piece of fir.

"Look out!" he called. "I'm going to push it off the shelf." So everyone looked out, and down came the little branch of fir tree, flopping down to the floor.

The wind-up sailor climbed down. He did a little dance of joy when he saw what a wonderful tree the bit of fir would make. He wondered what to put it in.

"If you'll get me out of my box, so that I can join in the fun for once, you can use my box," said the gruff voice of Jack-in-the-Box.

The toys didn't really like Jack-in-the-Box very much. He lived inside a square box, and when the box was opened he suddenly leaped out on a long spring, and frightened them very much. The wind-up sailor didn't really know if he wanted to get Jack out of his box.

"Come on – just this once,"
said Jack-in-the-Box.
"I promise to be good.
I'll perform in the circus,
and be funny if you like."

So Jack-in-the-Box
was taken out of his box
and he wobbled everywhere
on his long spring, enjoying
his freedom very much.

The box was just right for the Christmas tree. The wind-up sailor filled it with dirt that he took from the pot that held a big plant belonging to Miss Roundy. Then he planted the piece of fir tree in it.

"Now to decorate it!" he said. So he got some tiny colored candles and some bright beads out of the bead box, and some tinsel from the counter, and anything else he could think of – and the tree really began to look very beautiful!

"I can make a star to go on the top of the tree," said the teddy bear, and he ran off to find some silver paper.

"And now don't any of you look," said the sailor, "because I'm going to wrap presents for you – yes, a present for every single one of you!"

The circus was practicing hard. There were two wind-up clowns in the toy shop, so they were exactly right for the circus. They could go head-over-heels very fast.

"We need some horses," said the black monkey, who was very busy. "Pink cat, stop prowling around the cakes, and see how many horses you can find."

The roly-poly man said he wanted to be a clown, so the teddy bear made him a clown's hat, and let him roll around the ring, knocking people over. Jack-out-of-his-Box jumped around and wiggled his head on his long neck. He was really very funny.

The pink cat borrowed some horses from the soldiers and the farm. She led them down to the circus ring.

Noah arrived with his animals from the ark. There were elephants, lions, tigers, and even kangaroos!

"It's going to be a GRAND circus!" said the pink cat. "Oh, hurry up and come, Christmas Day!"

Well, Christmas Day did come at last! The toys ran to one another, shouting "Merry Christmas! Merry Christmas!" at the tops of their voices.

The wind-up train whistled its loudest. The big bear and the little bears pressed themselves in the middle and growled. The music box began to play, and the rag doll sat down at the toy piano and played a rollicking tune.

Nobody knew she could play, and they were all very surprised. So was the rag doll. She hadn't known either, and once she had begun to play she couldn't stop! So with the train's whistle, the bears' growling, the music box's tunes, and the piano there was a wonderful noise.

The roly-poly man got so excited that he knocked over two of the horses, rolled on the monkey's tail, and spilled a jug of lemonade.

"Can't you stop rolling around and be still for a moment?" said the pink cat, keeping her tail well out of the way.

"I can't stand still," said the roly-poly man, "because I've got something very heavy at the bottom of me. It makes me wobble, but not fall over. I really will try to be good – but if you were as wobbly as I am you'd find it difficult, too."

The black monkey suddenly appeared dressed up in white trousers and a top hat! He carried a whip in his hand. He cracked it and made everyone jump.

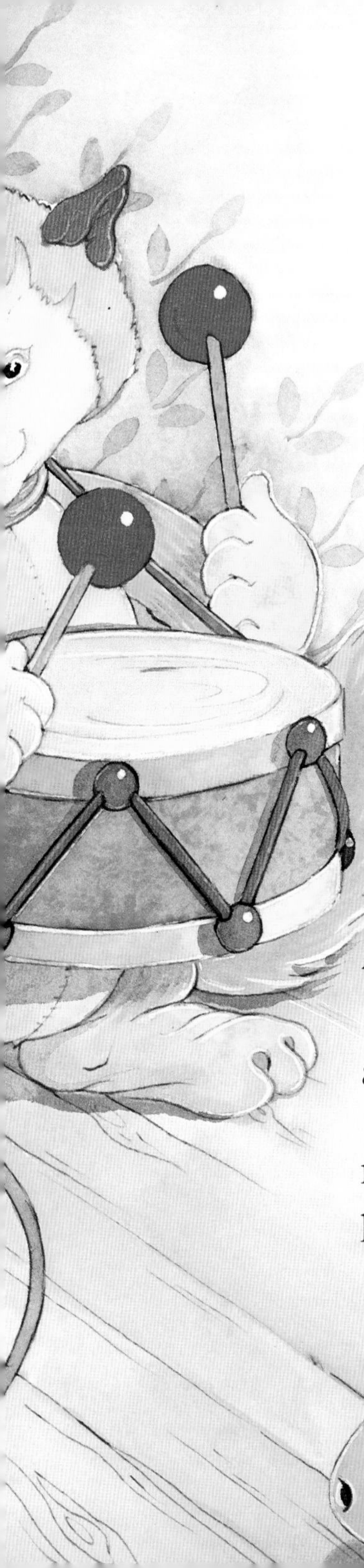

Then the pink cat appeared, carrying a drum. She beat it – boom-diddy-boom-diddy-boom-boom-boom.

"The circus is about to begin!" shouted the black monkey and he cracked his whip again. "Step right up, everyone! The circus is about to begin!"

"Boom-diddy-boom-diddy-boom!" went the drum.

All the toys rushed for seats. The black monkey had arranged blocks of all sizes and shapes out of the block-boxes for seats, and there was room for everyone. The doll house dolls were allowed to be at the front because they were so small.

The skittles were so excited that they kept giggling and falling over.

"Quiet there! Settle down please!" shouted the monkey. "Pink cat, sound the drum again – the performers are about to march in."

The circus began. You should have seen it! The horses were splendid. They ran around the ring one way, and then turned and went the other way.

Then the clowns came on, with Jack and the roly-poly man. The roly-poly man rolled all over the place and knocked all the clowns over. Then the clowns tried to catch Jack, but they couldn't, of course, because Jack sprang away from them on his long spring. The toys almost cried with laughter.

The elephants were cheered when they came in. They waved their trunks in the air and trumpeted as loudly as they could. The lions and tigers came in and roared fiercely. The kangaroos jumped all around the ring and the bears walked in standing up on their hind legs.

All the toys clapped and cheered and stamped at the end, and said it was the very best circus in the world. The pink cat and the black monkey felt very proud, and they stood in the middle of the ring and bowed to everyone so many times that they made their backs ache.

"Now for the tea party!" called the doll with golden hair. "Come along! You must be very hungry, toys – hurry up and come to the party!"

What a wonderful tea party it was! There were little tables everywhere. In the middle of them were vases of flowers that the dolls had picked out of the dolls' hats that Miss Roundy kept in a box on a special shelf.

The tables were set with the cups and saucers and plates out of the boxes of toy tea sets. There was a tea-pot on each, full of lemonade to pour into the cups.

The cakes were lovely. There were fudge cakes, peppermints, chocolate cakes, all kinds of cookies, toffee sandwiches, jelly candy that wobbled like the roly-poly man, and, of course, the Christmas cake was the best thing of all.

“We’ve put it on a table by itself, because it’s so big,” said the golden-haired doll. “I hope there will be a slice for everybody. Light the candles, twin dolls.”

The cake blazed up, all its tiny candles alight. It looked beautiful. The golden-haired doll had decorated it with icing. Everyone thought that was very clever.

The pink cat ate so much that she got fatter than ever. The captain of the soldiers lent the twin dolls his sharp sword to cut the cake. The roly-poly man rolled up to see them cutting it, and nearly got his head cut off!

When nobody could eat any more, and all the lemonade was drunk, the skittles cleared the tables. "We'll wash the dishes and put all the tea sets back in their boxes," they said. "The rest of you can play games."

So, while the skittles were busy, the toys played party games. They played blind man's buff, and the blindfolded pink cat caught the elephant from the Noah's Ark.

"Who can it be?" wondered the pink cat, feeling the elephant carefully. All the toys laughed, because of course, they knew who it was.

They played hunt the thimble, and nobody could see for a long time where the thimble was hidden. Then the wind-up sailor gave a scream.

"The captain of the soldiers is wearing it for a helmet – he is, he is!"

And so he was. He was sorry to give it up because he thought it was a very nice helmet.

The trains gave everyone rides, and so did the toy cars. Even the airplane said it would fly around the nursery once with everybody. The music box played hard for anyone who wanted to dance.

The roly-poly man made everyone laugh when he tried to dance with the rag doll. He rolled around so much that he knocked everyone off the floor.

They were all having such a good time. Then suddenly they noticed that all the candles on the Christmas tree were lighted!

"Oh, oh! It's time for the Christmas tree!" cried the toys, and they rushed over to it. "Isn't it pretty? Look at the star at the top!"

"Where's the wind-up sailor?" said the roly-poly man.

"Gone to get Santa Claus, he told me," said the rocking horse. "Do you suppose he meant it?"

And then, will you believe it, there came the noise of bells!

"Sleigh bells! It really is Santa Claus coming!" cried all the toys, and they rushed to the chimney. "He's coming! He's coming!"

Down the chimney came a pair of legs – then a pair of red pants – and then with a jump, down on the rug came a merry, white-whiskered fellow, whose red hood framed his jolly red face.

"Santa Claus! You've come, you've come!" shouted the toys, and dragged him to the tree.

"Wait a bit – I want my sack. It's just a little way up the chimney," said Santa Claus. So the big teddy bear got it. It was a nice big bumpy-looking sack.

"Merry Christmas, toys," said Santa Claus. He was a very nice *little* Santa Claus, not much bigger than the dolls. The toys were glad. They would have been afraid of a great big one.

"Merry Christmas!" sang out everyone. Then Santa Claus undid his bag. Oh, what a lot of things he had!

There were ribbons and necklaces for the dolls, candy for the soldiers, chocolates for the Noah's Ark animals, and balls, made of red holly berries, for the toy animals. Nobody had been forgotten. It was wonderful.

S.H.P.

Santa Claus handed out all the presents, beaming happily. Then he took a few presents from under the tree.

"These are special presents for the people who tried to make your Christmas so nice," he said. "Presents for the golden-haired doll and the twin dolls – and for the black monkey and the pink cat – here you are, special little presents for being kind and good."

"But what about the wind-up sailor?" said the rocking horse, at once. "He did the tree, you know. Have you forgotten him?"

"Where is he?" said Santa Claus.

Well, dear me, he wasn't there! Would you believe it?

"I saw him last," said the rocking horse. "He said he was going to get you, Santa Claus. *Didn't* he bring you?"

"Well, I'm here, aren't I?" said Santa Claus, and he laughed. "Dear me – it's sad there's no present for the wind-up sailor, but I don't think he'll mind at all."

The toys had opened all their presents. Somewhere a clock struck twelve. Midnight! Dear dear, how very late!

The twin dolls yawned loudly, and that made everyone yawn, too.

"We'd better clean up and go to bed," said the golden-haired doll. "Or we shall fall asleep on our feet, and that would never do."

So they cleaned up, and in the middle of it all Santa Claus disappeared. Nobody saw him go. The pink cat said she saw him go into the doll house, but he wasn't there when she looked.

Somebody else was, though – the wind-up sailor! The pink cat dragged him out.

"Here's the sailor!" she cried. "Here he is! Sailor, you missed Santa Claus – oh what a shame!"

But, you know, he didn't! He was there all the time. Have you guessed? He was Santa Claus, of course, all dressed up. He had climbed up the chimney when nobody was looking. Wasn't he clever?

"You were Santa Claus!" cried the golden-haired doll, and she hugged him hard. "You're a dear!"

"Yes, you are," shouted the rocking horse. "That was the best part of all, when Santa Claus came. We were so sad there was no present for you. But you will have one – you will, you will!"

And he did. The toys threaded a whole lot of red holly berries together and made him the finest necklace he had ever had. Look at him wearing it. Doesn't he look pleased?

Miss Roundy will never guess all that the toys did in her toy shop that Christmas Day, will she? If you ever meet her, you can tell her. I wish I'd been there to see it all, don't you?